This Little Tiger book belongs to:

_____

_____

_____

For Jazz
~ J T

LITTLE TIGER PRESS
1 The Coda Centre, 189 Munster Road,
London SW6 6AW
www.littletigerpress.com

First published in Great Britain 2003
This edition published 2003

Text copyright © Andrew Murray 2003
Illustrations copyright © Jack Tickle 2003
Andrew Murray and Jack Tickle have
asserted their rights to be identified as the
author and illustrator of this work under the
Copyright, Designs and Patents Act, 1988

All rights reserved • ISBN 978-1-85430-858-0

A CIP catalogue record for this book
is available from the British Library

Printed in China

3 4 5 6 7 8 9 10

The Very Sleepy Sloth

Andrew Murray

Jack Tickle

LITTLE TIGER PRESS

London

Deep in the jungle,
early in the morning,
the sloth was fast asleep.

But the rest of
the animals were
wide awake.

The cheetah was on the running machine, working on his

S P E E D.

The elephant was
lifting heavy weights,
working on her

STRENGTH.

The kangaroo was on the trampoline, working on her

SPRING.

S W I N G.

The monkey was
on the high bars,
working on his

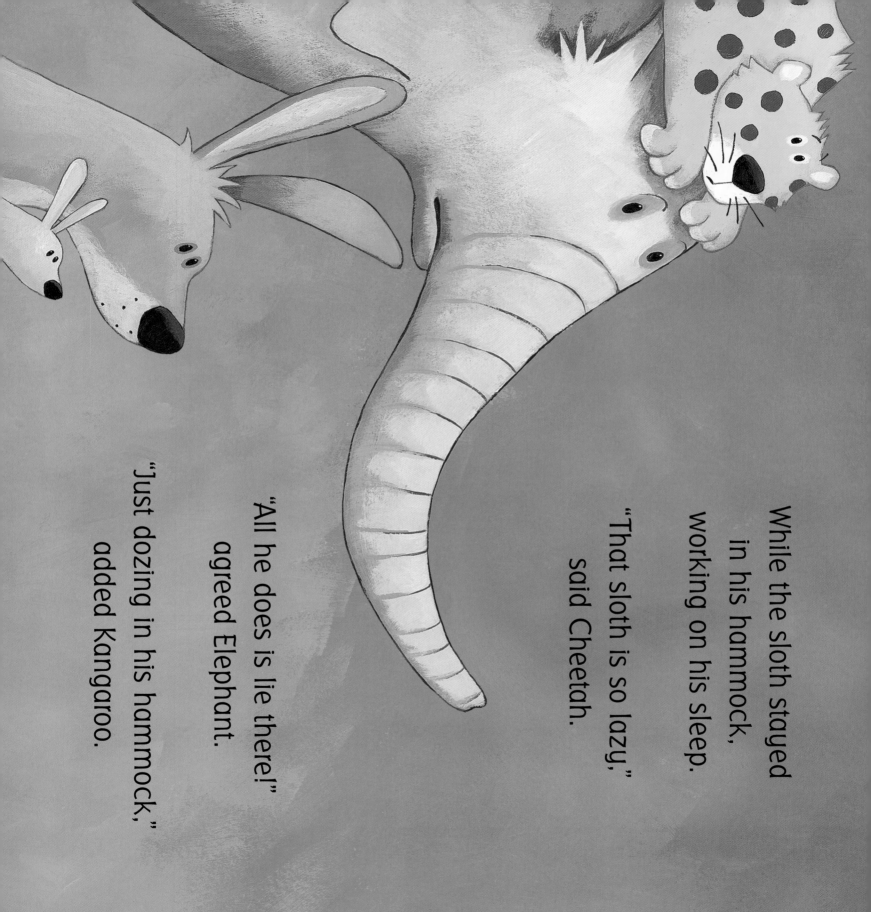

While the sloth stayed
in his hammock,
working on his sleep.

"That sloth is so lazy,"
said Cheetah.

"All he does is lie there!"
agreed Elephant.

"Just dozing in his hammock,"
added Kangaroo.

"Hey, Sloth!" called Monkey.
"We're all working hard here.
Why don't you get up and
do something?"

Sloth slowly opened one eye. "Monkey," he said. "If you're so hard-working, you try lifting Elephant's weights."

So Kangaroo tried
the running machine.
Cheetah chuckled as
Kangaroo landed on . . . .

. . . her bottom!

OOOOOOW!

"Cheetah!" said Kangaroo crossly. "If you're so clever, you swing like Monkey."

So Cheetah climbed the high bars and swung right into . . .

. . . Elephant.

EEEEEK . . !

By now, everyone was very hot, very tired and very, very, very cross.

"This is useless," they muttered. "Who caused all this trouble?"

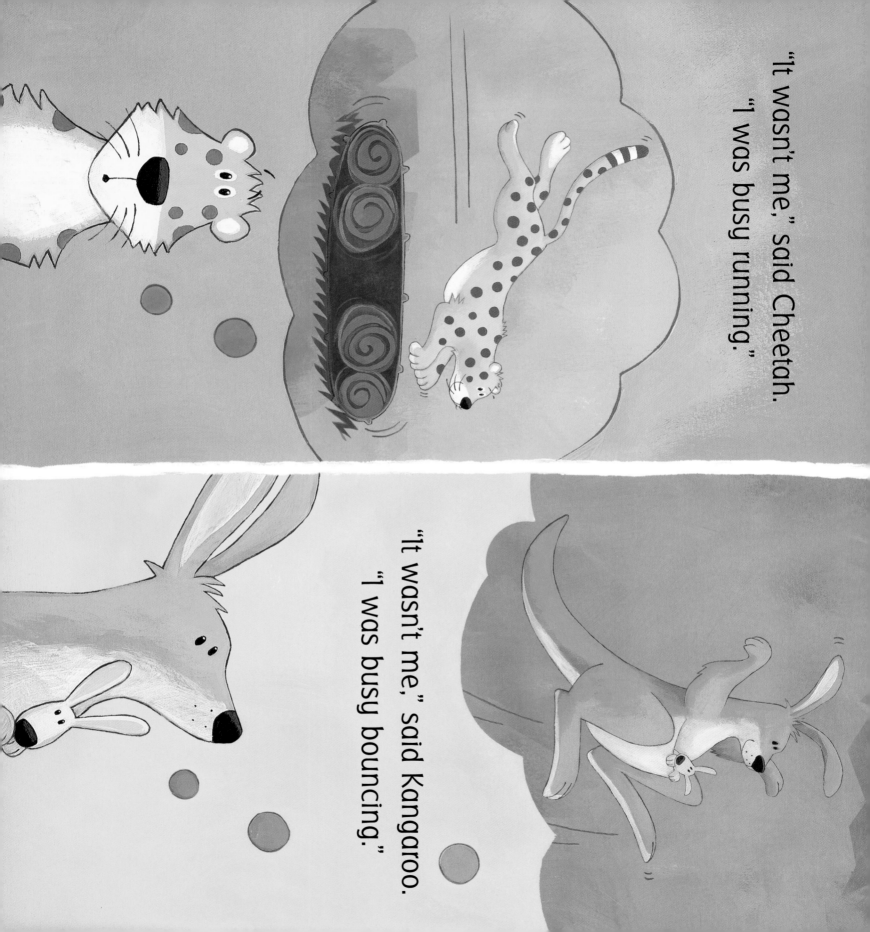

"And it wasn't me," said Monkey. "I was busy swinging." All the animals turned and looked at . . . .

"It wasn't me," said Elephant. "I was busy lifting weights."

SLOTH!

"Hey, Sloth," they called.
"You started this!"

Sloth turned lazily.

"You must see by now,"

he said. "We were all busy doing

what we do best. Even me!"

The animals thought about it.

"Yes!" they cried. "We're all good at

running or jumping or lifting or swinging.

But Sloth is the very best at . . .

"ZINE!"

"Exactly!" said Sloth.
And with a stretch
and a yawn he fell
fast asleep!